D0463657

THE
TENTH
INSIGHT:

Holding the Vision
A POCKET GUIDE

James Redfield

WARNER Ⓦ TREASURES ®
PUBLISHED BY WARNER BOOKS
A TIME WARNER COMPANY

FOR MY DAUGHTERS
MEGAN AND KELLY

UNDERSTANDING THE TRANSFORMATION

Throughout history, we humans have experienced dramatic shifts in how we have lived and viewed the world. One of the first such shifts occurred many thousands of years ago, when early mankind realized that they need not be confined to lives of wandering and gathering, struggling each day to find food. For thousands of years we had lived in small bands that could move quickly, each group canvassing the countryside, looking for berries, eatable roots, and wildlife that could be consumed for nourishment. When these foodstuffs were depleted, the band had no choice but to move on, for that was the only conceivable way of life.

Then slowly, we realized that we could cultivate certain plants and domesticate certain animals, making it possible to form villages and to settle permanently in one fertile region, storing our surplus foods. Because enough food could be provided without everyone working as farmers, other occupations emerged, and thus civilization was born. This transformation from wandering to farming villages dramatically changed the prevailing worldview and created a new vision of life unthinkable only a few centuries earlier.

A second major world transformation occurred a few thousand years later, as the complexity of civilization reached an even higher level. Powerful energy sources and advances in technology suddenly made it possible for the mass production of goods and services and increased mobility. Instead of each village supplying its own leather, metal, clothing, and shelter needs, these items suddenly could be created by a few people in some distant city. By mid-nineteenth century the great shift known as the Industrial Revolution had created a mass migration from the farms to the urban workplace. Suddenly, in one generation, the human ability to provide for our basic survival needs had escalated, and the enhanced economic security altered our worldview forever.

Many thinkers now believe we are on the brink of another equally significant shift in our worldview, one that transcends the secular and technological shifts of the past. The next great shift is philosophical and spiritual. We have raised our security level to a point where we can now fully look at the fact of our existence on this planet. We feel an urge to explore with greater depth the age-old questions of life. Why are we really here? Is there a spiritual purpose underlying the struggles of human history? Can we find an inner intuitive guidance for our lives that is truly spiritual?

As this century closes and we face not only a new hundred-year period but the beginning of a whole new millennium, the answers to many of these questions have begun to come in, penetrating our awareness through a series of archetypal insights—insights that are derived from the evidence of our own experience. Theses answers are forming a new cultural consensus about the nature of life and how to live it, creating a new spiritual vision for our time.

MOVING TOWARD
THE TENTH INSIGHT

For the emerging spiritual renaissance to fully arrive, the first nine Insights must not just become known but lived. We must wake up in the morning expecting exciting and mysterious coincidences to occur in our lives, and we must see these guiding coincidences as leading us somewhere. We must take these coincidences seriously (the Second Insight). We must treat the universe as the energy-filled place that it is, realizing that we are energy systems ourselves (the Third Insight). We must know that we humans often feel short of energy and seek to steal energy from others by dominating and creating conflict (the Fourth Insight). And to transcend this conflict, we must find our own source of this energy within, as the mystics of all religions advise (the Fifth Insight).

Once we find this inner energy, we have enough power to look closely at ourselves, discovering our control dramas, and going past them to ask, "What is my life about? What am I really supposed to be doing?" and finding our own individual sense of mission in the world (the Sixth Insight). This focuses the coincidences in our lives, and then we must use our intuition, our dreams, and our perception of light to increase the mysterious way our missions unfold so that we are placed perfectly to contribute to the world (the Seventh Insight), always uplifting others and utilizing the power of groups (the Eighth Insight). Then we must live with the knowledge that as we move forward, we are energizing our bodies to heightened degrees, evolving toward humanity's ultimate destiny: the spiritualization of our bodies and of all human culture on the planet (the Ninth Insight).

As we embrace these first nine Insights, I believe that we are bringing in a tenth, an insight that creates a wider perspective, a higher viewpoint for implementing the spiritual life on this planet—a viewpoint that comes from our growing awareness of the Afterlife dimension. Each month a host of new books, documentaries, and personal accounts move in front of us, and each month we know more about the spiritual life we were living before birth and the one to which we will return after death. It is this perspective that hastens the understanding that we are spiritual beings moving history in a particular direction. The Tenth Insight begins when we see this physical universe in a new name, and remember why we came.

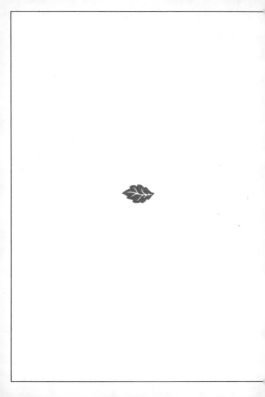

The Tenth Insight

SACRED
SITES

Always we must remember to return to the source. Everything depends on this reconnection—our strength, our love, our patience. We come to this Earth first to find the greater part of ourselves, the part that resides past simple ego and the struggle for survival. We then learn to look, ask, knock on the door, venture in search of that which is sacred.

When we venture into the unspoiled, timeless places where the processes of nature operate freely, we touch the sacred mystery of higher energy and eternity. These places are not just the heritage of our ancestors and the virgin world in which they lived, but are also sanctuaries that belong to our children and to their children. They are natural resources to be walked and photographed and conserved, places of peace and solitude that remind us who we are.

Yet every remaining natural site needs to be protected, since those who are still asleep are reducing these sacred, cathedral sites to mere lumber products or agricultural plots. Like prodigal children, we must return to this source or depth of being, knowing that we are no longer part of the forces of greed and error that would destroy these special places.

We are more. We are part of the love that opens our hearts to clear any distractions and opens every door so that our message can touch the world. And these sites are reservoirs of divine energy from which we can drink daily.

A GIFT
FROM THE ANIMALS

Even as our few remaining wilderness areas are threatened, each day more of us venture into these beautiful landscapes to experience the energy for ourselves. And, immersed in the natural rhythms of the earth and the wind and the sky, our minds relax and we view our lives with quiet perspective. We can see our paths and can recognize the synchronicity that has guided our footsteps. Suddenly, we begin to experience another kind of mysterious occurrence: the presence of animals.

As we walk through these natural settings, animals will appear at certain times, as if to highlight our thoughts and to validate our deepest intuitions. Each species presents a different message as the creatures linger, revealing themselves. If we watch carefully and spiritually, identifying with their movement and focus, we can remember an aspect of ourselves long forgotten. We suddenly sense new abilities of perception, discernment—an approach to life that we need, miraculously, at this very point in our life's journey.

The appearance of these creatures is a reminder of who we are, of the consciousness we have known and lost and are ready to embrace again. We have only to protect the wilderness and then to enter its sacred world with alertness and respect. There the truth of how to approach our lives, how to handle any situation, will come to us—a gift from the animals.

The Tenth Insight

BELIEVING IN
OUR INTUITIONS

As we stay connected with the divine source within and become more observant of the mysterious coincidences guiding our lives, we begin to perceive the exact way this experience flows. We realize that our intuitions, which we first notice as hunches and inner feelings, become visible as fleeting images, pictures in the back of our minds of ourselves doing something or going somewhere. They are potential paths that we can take in the future.

Yet we can easily dismiss our intuitions as random thoughts, wishful thinking, or fantasy. Our own skepticism or doubt can erode the power of these images, sabotaging any synchronicity before it begins. Our challenge is to remain ever watchful for our intuitions and to hold their images in our mind. As long as we stay connected with our inner source of love, they will always be reliable, helpful to others, and oriented toward what we can contribute. Our intuitions become our road maps into the future.

We need to hold these images with our whole heart, and when we do—when we give them priority—events magically begin to unfold. This doesn't mean that the images won't be vague. They will be. And it doesn't mean that we won't "hit brick walls." That will happen. But if we stay committed to the process, the next intuition will clarify where we are going and help us around any obstacle.

The Tenth Insight

OVERCOMING
THE FEAR

Since the beginning of human experience, isolation—and the fear that it brings—has been our enemy. When we shut ourselves off from our inner source of love and happiness, we can lapse into a posture of despair and feelings of futility toward life. We then easily focus on the negatives of existence: the poverty, the violence and hatred, the disease in our world.

The great truth surfacing in Western culture is that we don't need to be slaves to our emotions. Regardless of our external situation, we can connect with a deeper source that brings our emotions back to the only true emotion in the state of connectedness: love.

Once we are imbued with this love, it

becomes our primary feeling toward life. From it emerges a call to action, an inspiration that becomes the central focus of how we want to spend our lives, what we want to do. The more we stay in this love, the more we become aware of the fear and the resentments that sometimes block it and interrupt our health and energy.

If we try to remember the origins of these fears and resentments, we can clear them and open again to the power of divine connection. We can stay focused on our special mission in the world. By holding to our inspiration, we can transform our lives and energize our bodies—since true health comes from remembering who we are and fully engaging in our spiritual purpose.

The Tenth Insight

A KNOWLEDGE OF
THE AFTERLIFE

Slowly, year by year, our minds have been opened to the wider context of human life on this planet. For centuries, life was reduced to what could be proved by a materialistic science. Being alive was considered principally in terms of material survival and prosperity.

We easily slipped into a certain obsessiveness, driven by our work and by the social need to gain recognition and status from being "successful." We focused on making the world more materially abundant, and we thought of little else. Even our religions reduced what had been a spiritual experience to a material conception of belief and creed and ideology, rarely considering our spiritual nature.

But then science itself began to change, and finally its message has begun to be filtered into the mass consciousness of our society: that human beings have systematically encountered a range of experience that doesn't fit into the materialistic paradigm. We slowly began to talk about these experiences.

In "near death" encounters, people have glimpsed and even explored the region we now call the Afterlife. Now we others can begin to explore its shape and its way of life. It is evidence of our true spiritual nature that at once calms our minds and spiritualizes our earthly existence.

The Tenth Insight

ANGELS
IN OUR MIDST

One of the lasting effects of the heightened conversation about our spiritual experiences is our growing belief in angels and other spiritual guides. As our culture has become more comfortable and open about paranormal perceptions, more and more people are talking about their experiences with angels.

From the people who have had "near-death" experiences, we hear about a range of encounters with spiritual entities in the Afterlife who act as guides and special advisers. These entities usually explain the near-death experience and help the person encountering death to assess his or her life, formulate his or her mission, and sometimes decide whether or not to return to the Earthly dimension. Often this relationship with the guide continues upon the person's return.

Just as amazing are the many stories of angel intervention in this dimension, as told by those whose lives have been touched by these celestial beings. Visitations can occur during the day or night, in or outside of our homes—but always the angel brings a message of importance that transforms us.

The Tenth Insight

THE LIFE
REVIEW

One of the most pervasive and constant elements of the near-death experience is the Life Review. Usually, the person undergoing the experience is taken to a place permeated with pleasing white light. There, he or she is greeted by knowledgeable spiritual beings or by relatives. Feeling immensely comfortable, protected, and loved, the person begins to see a vision of his or her life, beginning with birth and proceeding forward to the present. For most people, this vision is seen in remarkable detail, focusing on our emotional encounters with others and how our own behavior affected them.

These reviews can be extremely unpleasant, revealing how we may have negatively impacted the feelings of others. On the other hand, we also see the positive effects of our actions on Earth—the times we uplifted another or helped another with a life difficulty. Often, those who have undergone such a review come back with a renewed sense of what they want to do with their lives and a knowledge of the behaviors and tendencies that they must overcome.

Life Reviews are transforming, describing not only what we all will face at the end of our current lives but also a process in which we can engage before our bodies die. We can review our actions now and renew ourselves. We can be born in a truer sense and pursue life with a new purpose.

REMEMBERING
OUR INTENTION

As our trust of the spiritual increases, we step back and comprehend our experiences of intuition and coincidence. When seemingly incredible coincidences occur to lead us forward, we perceive that these poignant moments are somehow predestined.

It could be the meeting of a new person, the discovery of a new job or project, or the decision to move to a new place. In all of these instances, we sense an inevitability in what is occurring. Our consciousness expands, and we intuitively know that these events are unfolding as they are meant to unfold.

Suddenly, great blocks of our personal histories—the vague twists and turns, the incomprehensible stumbling blocks, the almost obsessive need at times to explore certain information or to understand the work of a particular individual—begin to make sense. Everything that has happened in the past has been in preparation for today—a long road conveying us to this exact moment.

With this clarity, our consciousness expands. We realize that long ago we foresaw these events. We hoped for them. We planned to come into this life with certain interests and momentum so that we could eventually awaken and accomplish a special purpose. We came here wishing to follow a certain path of preparation and then, finally, to remember fully a message we intended to bring into the world—which is a personal truth that only we can tell.

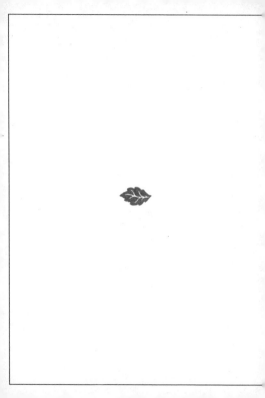

The Tenth Insight

A HISTORY OF
AWAKENING

As we begin to remember that special truth we are here to tell, we see the great span of human history as a context, a long narrative of progress within which our own lives are unfolding. Our task is to slowly wake up and to realize that life is not just about survival but also about spiritual evolution.

This spiritual evolution explains why our ancestors gave up wandering in small bands and intuited that we could cultivate plants and herd livestock. It explains why we were inwardly guided toward industrialization and technology. It explains why we developed more democratic ways of interacting and higher ethical standards of true relationship. And it explains why we now have the need to focus more intently on each interpersonal encounter.

Today we are aware of an underlying spiritual dynamic hidden in each human contact, no matter how fleeting that contact might be. Such encounters shift our creativity and productivity to maximum levels of efficiency. We are inspired by the deeper spiritual messages coming from those who spontaneously enter our lives.

Suddenly, our own truths make sense. Each of us has a special contribution to make that reflects the greater movement of history. We are all involved in moving human culture forward, but our missions are synchronistic with a larger evolutionary step that we all sense.

Our highest truths today serve to inwardly transform our industrialized world to make it more compatible and sustainable within the larger natural environment. We are moving to automate our technological world, shifting the focus of our lives to the greater adventure of spiritual growth.

The Tenth Insight

FACING THE
POLARIZATION

From the perspective of the Afterlife—that place to which our memories stretch the furthest and from which we can see the long narrative of history as spiritual awakening—the purpose and destiny of humankind seem clear.

Each historical milestone, each evolutionary step, brings more spiritual knowledge into the physical plane. As this continues to occur, we live a deeper spirituality, integrating it into our beings, lightening our bodies. For most of us, intuiting our ultimate destiny of becoming true spirits comes easily. Eventually, we all will exist in a spiritual culture here on Earth, aligned with God's Heaven.

But to evolve into a true spiritual culture, we must first move away from the materialistic worldview that has characterized the last four centuries. And for some of us, this is difficult. The materialistic worldview seems safe and familiar and allows us to repress the anxieties of life. The great mystery of existence is reduced to mere routines of daily living, to an economic and financial struggle for survival.

Questions about being, death, the Afterlife, and God are pushed aside and barely considered. In order to push these questions out of our minds, we who insist on discussing them are criticized and discredited. As spiritual insight on our planet increases, a great polarization is becoming evident. On one side are those who sense and believe in the spiritual renaissance. On the other are those who resist it, who feel that certain traditions are being left behind. Only love and open discourse can ease this tension and ensure that the best expression of what is true emerges.

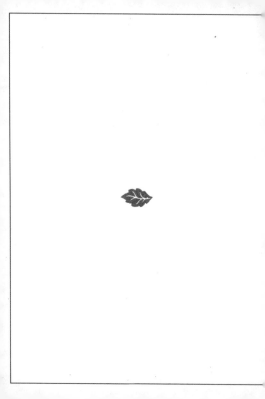

The Tenth Insight

HOLDING
THE VISION

If we are to truly incorporate into our daily lives this emerging spiritual renaissance, we need to adopt the highest ethic in envisioning the future. And if our intuitions are correct, we must believe in the guiding process of synchronicity.

We need to understand that mysterious coincidences will continue to move us through the Insights—so that we can clear our egos and become aware that each of our lives has been in preparation to make a special contribution to the world. If we stay connected to the divine, we will remember with increasing clarity how to enact and fulfill our missions.

As our memories expand, we will meet others whom we sense we have known before. If we are able to work through any past resentments, we will find that their missions are synchronistic with our own. Together we can begin to transform our daily work toward an overall mission of service. We will begin to sense not only each of our individual historical missions but the original plan—envisioned by us all somewhere long ago—for human history and experience.

It is this World Vision—the future that we all are here to enact—that will motivate millions of visionaries to solve the world's great social problems of pollution, crime, war, and poverty, and to establish this new spiritual culture in our physical plane.

To be achieved, this World Vision must

be remembered and communicated by increasingly more people. We must uplift everyone, help them to remember, treat no one as an enemy. We must each make a choice about the future we envision. And we must hold this Vision to save our world.

INFORMATION
FROM THE AUTHOR

A monthly newsletter is available from the author on the ideas brought forth in *The Celestine Prophecy* and *The Tenth Insight*. "The Celestine Journal" chronicles the author's present experiences and reflections on the spiritual renaissance occurring on our planet. Subscription rates are $29.95 for one year from Sartori Publishing, P.O. Box 360988, Hoover, Alabama 35236.

Warner Books is not responsible for the delivery or content of the information or materials provided by the author. The reader should address any questions to the author at the above address.